Bottoms Up!

Jokes from Bikini Bottom

by David Lewman
illustrated by Caleb Meurer

Based on the TV series SpongeBob SquarePants created by Stephen Hillenburg as seen on Nickelodeon.

First published in Great Britain in 2004 by Simon & Schuster UK Ltd,
Africa House, 64-78 Kingsway, London WC2B 6AH

Originally published in the USA in 2002 by Simon Spotlight,
an imprint of Simon & Schuster Children's Division, New York.

A CIP catalogue record for this book is available from the British Library

ISBN 0689874936

Printed in China
1 3 5 7 9 10 8 6 4 2

Why did SpongeBob and Patrick climb onto the fishermens' lines?

They were playing hooky.

Why did Patrick bring nose plugs to go jellyfishing?

He thought they were going smellyfishing.

BZzz

BZZz

Why did SpongeBob bring musical instruments to Jellyfish Fields?

What is Sandy's favourite carnival ride?

The Tilt-a-Squirrel.